MEMORY JARS

VERA BROSGOL

blueberry
jam

Roaring Brook Press
New York

On a hot, sweet, sticky July day, Freda went blueberry picking with her gran.

Deep among the bushes full of fat blue fruit, Freda ate as many as she picked.

They tasted like sweet sunshine.

They were the best right then,
and they'd never be better.

She ate until her fingertips were
purple and her stomach felt like
a giant blueberry.

But still there were so many left.

"I can't do it! I can't eat them all!" moaned Freda.

"Calm down, French Fry," said Gran. "We can put them in a jar and save them.

"I use them for my special jam every year.
It was your grandpa's favorite recipe."

Freda remembered her grandpa eating toast
every morning with glossy, purple jam on it . . .

. . . making sure it was spread all the way
to the crust so every last bite was sweet.

Freda remembered her grandpa.

"So if we save the berries in jars, they'll be just as good?" asked Freda.

"Yes," said Gran. "The jars keep them preserved for a long time, so we can eat blueberries in January if we like!"

Freda had an idea.

She tried her idea out on one of Gran's fresh chocolate chip cookies.

It was very, very hard not to eat it.

She put the cookie jar under her bed,
said good night to Gran . . .

. . . and sort of slept.

she checked . . .

. . . and it had worked.

The cookie would be warm and yummy forever.

She had saved it.

Freda wondered what
else she could save.

She was going to need a lot more jars.

Freda saved all kinds of things:

HALLOWEEN CANDY

WARM COOKIE

NEW STUFFED ANIMAL (TAG STILL ON)

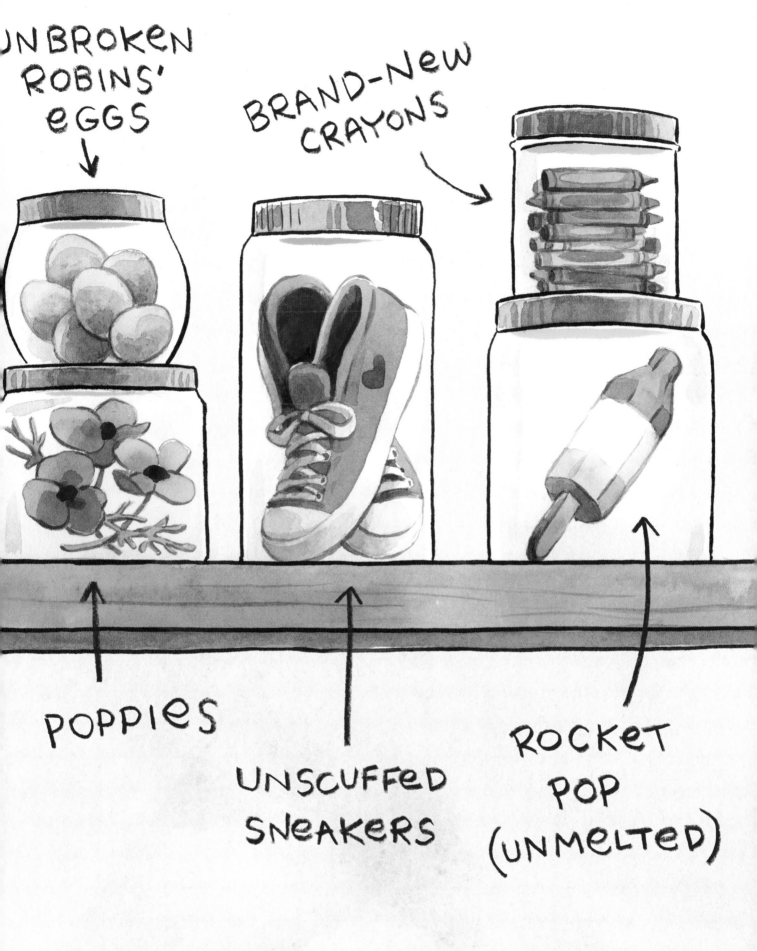

Freda didn't want Jack, her best friend on the entire planet, to move to Arizona at the end of the month.

Neither did he.

And now he wouldn't.

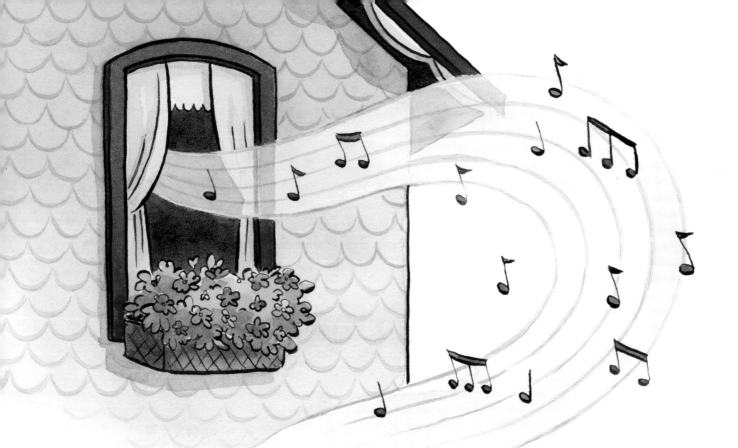

Mrs. Alexander's beautiful singing voice drifted over the
neighborhood, as it did every Saturday afternoon . . .

. . . straight into one of Freda's jars, where
the song would live, safe and never-ending.

The cloud that looked just like a unicorn would never be pushed back into a mushy nothing by the wind.

The laser-bright rainbow would never dim as the sun moved.

The full moon, her favorite shape, would never fade away and leave the sky empty and dark, making Freda feel alone.

She took the stars while she was at it.

Finally, Freda's favorite things were tucked away in jars.

Everything would
be saved and safe,
just the same,
forever.

Almost everything.

"Please?"

"Well all right, French Fry.
Anything you like."

The neighborhood was very quiet
as Freda and Gran went home.

All that saving had made Freda hungry.

The toast was warm
and crunchy . . .

. . . but it was
missing something.

Something sweet.

She spread the jam all
the way to the edges.

It tasted like . . .

. . . Freda remembered.

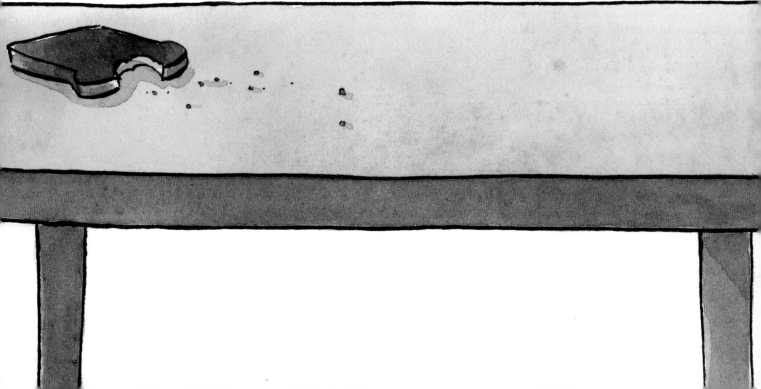

On a cold, blustery day in December,
Freda had breakfast with her gran.

"Whoops! We ran out
of jam," said Gran.

"Don't worry," said Freda.
"We can make more next summer."

Then she took a bite. It was delicious.
Just like she remembered.

The end?

BLUEBERRY JAM

This recipe involves some cooking, so make sure you have an adult to help!

YOU WILL NEED:

- 6 cups blueberries, rinsed
- 3 cups sugar
- 2 tablespoons fresh lemon juice
- ¾ teaspoon cinnamon
- ¼ teaspoon nutmeg
- 2 pint jars with lids

SMUSH
SMUSH

 1 Put your berries in a bowl and mush them up! (This part is pretty fun.) Leave some whole if you like chunky jam.

 2 Pour the berry mush into a pot with the sugar. With an adult's help, turn the stove on to medium-high and let the mush come to a boil. Cook for a few minutes, then lower the heat.

3 Simmer for about 15 minutes, stirring often. While the jam is cooking, warm your jars, either in some hot water in the sink or by putting them in the oven at 200 degrees F.

4 Stir in the lemon juice, cinnamon, and nutmeg. Keep cooking the jam till it's shiny and thick, about 8 minutes. It should gloop off the spoon.

5 Once the jam is thick enough, use a ladle to pour it into your warmed-up jars. A funnel will help! Try not to lick the spoon—it's hot.

6 Let the jars cool till they're safe to touch, then put the lids on.

7 Now you can lick the spoon.

Blueberry jam

Blueberry jam

8 Put your jars in the fridge and enjoy them for a few weeks (if they last that long). The jam tastes best when shared with someone you love.

For
Judy

Copyright © 2021 by Vera Brosgol • Published by Roaring Brook Press • Roaring Brook Press is a division of Holtzbrinck Publishing Holdings Limited Partnership
120 Broadway, New York, NY 10271 • mackids.com • All rights reserved. • Library of Congress Cataloging-in-Publication Data • Names: Brosgol, Vera, author,
illustrator • Title: Memory jars / Vera Brosgol. • Description: First edition. | New York, NY : Roaring Brook Press, 2021. | Audience: Ages 4–8. | Audience:
Grades K–1. | Summary: Freda uses jars to save everything from a chocolate chip cookie to the full moon, just as her grandmother saves summer blueberries.
Includes a recipe for blueberry jam. • Identifiers: LCCN 2020039816 | ISBN 9781250314871 (hardcover) • Subjects: CYAC: Collectors and collecting—Fiction.
| Food—Preservation—Fiction. | Grandmothers—Fiction. | Jam—Fiction. • Classification: LCC PZ7.1.B788 Mem 2021 | DDC [E]—dc23 • LC record available at
https://lccn.loc.gov/2020039816 • Our books may be purchased in bulk for promotional, educational, or business use. Please contact your local bookseller or the
Macmillan Corporate and Premium Sales Department at (800) 221-7945 ext. 5442 or by email at MacmillanSpecialMarkets@macmillan.com. • First edition, 2021
Book design by Jen Keenan • This book was drawn with dip pen and acrylic ink and painted in watercolor, with some Adobe Photoshop shenanigans afterward.
Printed in China by RR Donnelley Asia Printing Solutions Ltd., Dongguan City, Guangdong Province • 10 9 8 7 6 5